-Read Book

oween,
Dear Dragon

by Margaret Hillert
Illustrated by Jack Pullan

NORWOOD HOUSE 🏠 PRESS

DEAR CAREGIVER,

The books in this Beginning-to-Read collection may look somewhat familiar in that the original versions could have been a part of your own early reading experiences. These carefully written texts feature common sight words to provide your child multiple exposures to the words appearing most frequently in written text. These new versions have been updated and the engaging illustrations are highly appealing to a contemporary audience of young readers.

Begin by reading the story to your child, followed by letting him or her read familiar words and soon your child will be able to read the story independently. At each step of the way, be sure to praise your reader's efforts to build his or her confidence as an independent reader. Discuss the pictures and encourage your child to make connections between the story and his or her own life. At the end of the story, you will find reading activities and a word list that will help your child practice and strengthen beginning reading skills. These activities, along with the comprehension questions are aligned to current standards, so reading efforts at home will directly support the instructional goals in the classroom.

Above all, the most important part of the reading experience is to have fun and enjoy it!

Shannon Cannon

Shannon Cannon,
Literacy Consultant

Norwood House Press • www.norwoodhousepress.com
Beginning-to-Read™ is a registered trademark of Norwood House Press.
Illustration and cover design copyright ©2017 by Norwood House Press. All Rights Reserved.

LIBRARY OF CONGRESS CATALOGING-IN-PUBLICATION DATA

Names: Hillert, Margaret, author. I Pullan, Jack, illustrator.
Title: It's Halloween, Dear Dragon / by Margaret Hillert ; illustrated by Jack Pullan.
Other titles: It is Halloween, Dear Dragon
Description: Chicago, IL : Norwood House Press, [2016] I Series: A
  beginning-to-read book I Summary: "A boy and his pet dragon enjoy fall
  activities and celebrate Halloween. Completely re-illustrated from
  original edition. Title also includes reading activities and a word
  list"-- Provided by publisher.
Identifiers: LCCN 2015046743 (print) I LCCN 2016014727 (ebook) I ISBN
  9781599537733 (library edition : alk. paper) I ISBN 9781603578998 (eBook)
Subjects: I CYAC: Halloween--Fiction. I Dragons--Fiction.
Classification: LCC PZ7.H558 It 2016 (print) I LCC PZ7.H558 (ebook) I DDC
  [E]--dc23
LC record available at http://lccn.loc.gov/2015046743

288N—072016
Manufactured in the United States of America in North Mankato, Minnesota.

Look up here.
Do you see what I see?
Something red.
Something yellow.

3

And look down here.
We can play here.
This is fun.

See what I can do.
I can make you look funny.
Oh, oh, oh.
Funny, funny you.

I can work, too.
Work, work, work.
I can help Father.

Come here.
Come here.
You can work, too.
You can help do this.

Now come with me.
I want to get something.
You can help.
Run, run, run.

Here is a big one.
We want this one.
And a little one, too.

Father, Father.
Look what we have.
Can you help us make something?

I can. I can.
I can do it.
Look at this.
Do you like this?

And look at this one.
I can make it funny.
It looks like you.

Here, little one.
Come up here.
This is something funny.
Do you want to see this?

Mother, Mother.
Can you make something, too?
Can you make something for us?

Yes, I can.
I can make something good.
You will like it.

Look at me.
See what I have.
Guess who I am.
Guess, guess.

We will go in here.
This will be fun.

Not you.
Not you.
No, you will not do.

23

Here.
You are the one.
Here is something for you.
You are funny.

Oh, my.
What do I see?
What do you have here?

Look what we can do.
Away we go.
Up, up, and away!
What a good ride.

Here you are with me.
And here I am with you.
Oh, what a happy Halloween,
Dear Dragon.

READING REINFORCEMENT

The following activities support the findings of the National Reading Panel that determined the most effective components for reading instruction are: Phonemic Awareness, Phonics, Vocabulary, Fluency, and Text Comprehension.

Phonemic Awareness: The /h/ sound

Sound Substitution: Say the words on the left to your child. Ask your child to repeat the word, changing the first sound to /**h**/:

pot = hot	book = hook	seal = heal
card = hard	sit = hit	ball = hall
nose = hose	tip = hip	jam = ham

Phonics: The letter Hh

1. Demonstrate how to form the letters **H** and **h** for your child.

2. Have your child practice writing **H** and **h** at least three times each.

3. Ask your child to point to the words in the book that begin with the letter **h**.

4. Write down the following words and ask your child to write the letter **h** in front of them to make a new word:

__air	__and	__eat	__old
__eel	__ear	__is	__ill

5. Read the words aloud. Ask your child to read all the words he or she knows.

Vocabulary: Contractions

1. Explain to your child that sometimes we combine two words to make one shorter word and that these new words are called contractions.

2. Point to the word **It's** on the front cover. Ask your child to name the two words that make **It's**. If your child doesn't know, explain that the word **It's** comes from the two words **it** and **is**.

3. Say the following contractions and ask your child to name the words that make each one:

don't	she's	can't	he'll	we've
I'll	doesn't	you're	isn't	they're

4. Write the following contractions and word pairs on separate pieces of paper.

did not / didn't	we will / we'll	are not / aren't
was not / wasn't	that is / that's	I am / I'm
we are / we're	you will / you'll	did not / didn't
you are / you're	let us / let's	it will / it'll

5. Ask your child to match the word pairs with the contractions they make.

Fluency: Shared Reading

1. Reread the story to your child at least two more times while your child tracks the print by running a finger under the words as they are read. Ask your child to read the words he or she knows with you.

2. Reread the story taking turns, alternating readers between sentences or pages.

Text Comprehension: Discussion Time

1. Ask your child to retell the sequence of events in the story.

2. To check comprehension, ask your child the following questions:

   • How did the boy and Dear Dragon help Father?

   • What did Father do with the pumpkins?

   • How did the boy make the jack-o-lantern look like Dear Dragon?

   • Which parts of the story could really happen? Which parts are make believe?

   • What do you do to celebrate Halloween?

WORD LIST

It's Halloween, Dear Dragon uses the 65 words listed below.
This list can be used to practice reading the words that appear in the text. You may wish to write the words on index cards and use them to help your child build automatic word recognition. Regular practice with these words will enhance your child's fluency in reading connected text.

a	Father	I	oh	up
am	for	in	one	us
and	fun	is		
are	funny	it	play	want
at				we
away	get	like	red	what
	go	little	ride	who
be	good	look (s)	run	will
big	guess			with
		make	see	work
can	Halloween	me	something	
come	happy	Mother		yellow
	have	my	the	yes
dear	help		this	you
do	here	no	to	
down		not	too	
dragon		now		

ABOUT THE AUTHOR Margaret Hillert has helped millions of children all over the world learn to read independently. She was a first grade teacher for 34 years and during that time started writing books that her students could both gain confidence in reading and enjoy. She wrote well over 100 books for children just learning to read. As a child, she enjoyed writing poetry and continued her poetic writings as an adult for both children and adults.

Photograph by Glenna Washburn

ABOUT THE ILLUSTRATOR A talented and creative illustrator, Jack Pullan, is a graduate of William Jewell College. He has also studied informally at Oxford University and the Kansas City Art Institute. He was mentored by the renowned watercolor artists, Jim Hamil and Bill Amend. Jack's work has graced the pages of many enjoyable children's books, various educational materials, cartoon strips, as well as many greeting cards. Jack currently resides in Kansas.